THE BEST-LOVED DOLL

THE BEST

Henry Holt and Company • *New York*

LOVED DOLL

Rebecca Caudill
Illustrated by Elliott Gilbert

Henry Holt and Company, LLC
Publishers since 1866
175 Fifth Avenue
New York, New York 10010
www.HenryHoltKids.com

Library of Congress Cataloging-in-Publication Data
Caudill, Rebecca.
The best-loved doll / Rebecca Caudill; illustrated by Elliott Gilbert
Originally published: New York: Holt, Rinehart and Winston, 1962.
Summary: For a doll contest at a party, a girl chooses to enter a
doll that seems least likely to win a prize.
ISBN 978-0-8050-5467-5
[1. Dolls—Fiction. 2. Contests—Fiction.] I. Gilbert, Elliott, ill. II. Title.
PZ7.C274Be   1992   [E]—dc20   92-898

First published in hardcover in 1962 by Holt, Rinehart and Winston
Reissued in hardcover 1992 by Henry Holt and Company
First paperback edition, 1997
Printed in July 2010 in China by South China Printing Company Ltd.,
Dongguan City, Guangdong Province, on acid-free paper. ∞
15 14 13 12

For Ann Elizabeth,
whose mother will tell
her just how it happened

The four dolls waited quietly, and listened.

Melissa sat upright in her cradle.

Belinda stood on the low bookshelf.

Mary Jane sat beside her.

Across Betsy's bed lay Jennifer.

They had been waiting ever since Betsy went downstairs to breakfast.

They had been waiting a long time.

When the clock struck eight, they heard Betsy's father leaving for his office.

When the clock struck nine, they heard Betsy's mother talking on the telephone.

When the clock struck ten, they heard the postman coming up the walk.

Five minutes later, they heard feet running up the stairs, fast.

"Here she comes!" cried Jennifer.

"Running like a rabbit!" wheezed Melissa.

Into the room ran Betsy. In her hand she held a piece of pink paper.

"Listen to this, dolls!" said Betsy. "It's an invitation to a party at Susan Anderson's house."

She read from the paper.

Bring one doll
to my party
this afternoon at four.
Prizes will be given for
the oldest doll,
the best-dressed doll,
the doll who can do the most things.

Betsy stared at the invitation. "Bring one doll," she read again.

She puckered her forehead.

"Which doll shall I take?" she asked.

She looked at Melissa.

"The oldest doll?"

She looked at Belinda.

"The best-dressed doll?"

She looked at Mary Jane.

"The doll who can do the most things?"

Then she looked at Jennifer. "Jennifer . . ." she said.

"Betsy!" called her mother.

"Coming!" called Betsy.

And down the stairs she ran.

Once more the room was quiet.

"A party!" sighed Belinda. "I wonder what you do at a party."

"You play games," said Mary Jane. "Remember when Betsy came home from the last party? She hid us all in the closet and then found us again."

"Hide-and-seek was the name of that game," said Melissa.

"You eat cake at parties," said Mary Jane. "Remember Betsy brought us a pinch of cake from the last party? Wrapped in a pink paper napkin?"

"You eat candy, too," said Jennifer. "Betsy's fingers were sticky with candy when she came home from the last party. My hair is still a little sticky where she brushed her hands across it."

"Sometimes you get a present," said Melissa. "Remember the time Betsy brought home that little red dog that lies on the shelf in the closet?" Melissa shuddered. "I never liked dogs," she said.

"But puppies can be fun," said Jennifer. "One day, when Betsy was holding me near the window, I could see a puppy chasing a squirrel up a tree."

"I shouldn't like to be chased," said Melissa.

"Not even if you weren't so old?" asked Belinda.

"And stiff in your joints?" asked Mary Jane.

"Not even if I weren't so old and stiff in my joints," said Melissa. "I shouldn't like to be chased."

"Oh," sighed Belinda, "I do hope Betsy takes me to that party! The invitation said, 'Bring your best-dressed doll.' Look at the beautiful clothes I'm wearing. And I have a trunkful of others besides."

"You do have beautiful clothes, Belinda," said Jennifer.

"Betsy ought to make a new dress for you, Jennifer," said Belinda. "That dress you are wearing is a fright."

Jennifer's dress was blue with white dots. It was the only dress she had ever had. She had worn it all of her life. It was faded and rumpled.

"I guess it is a fright," said Jennifer, smiling. "I hadn't thought about it before."

"My hearing's not good lately," complained Melissa. "But I thought I heard Betsy read, 'Bring your oldest doll.' If Betsy wants to win a prize, she'll take me to the party. I'm a hundred years old. I belonged to Betsy's great-great-grandmother."

"My! My! You really are old, Melissa," said Jennifer. "I'm only five."

"Pardon me for saying so, Jennifer dear," wheezed Melissa, "but you look to be five hundred."

Jennifer smiled. "That's because I've played so hard all my life," she said.

Jennifer lay across Betsy's bed trying to think of
something she could do. She smiled at Mary Jane.
   "You do smile prettily, Jennifer," Mary Jane told
her. "It's too bad you can do nothing else."

"You're forgetting," said Mary Jane, "that the invitation said, 'Bring the doll who can do the most things.' If Betsy wants a prize, she'll take me. What other doll can do the things I do? Tell me."

The dolls heard footsteps on the stairs.
"Here she comes!" cried Jennifer.

Betsy hurried into the room. She stood looking at
Melissa, at Belinda, and at Mary Jane.
She puckered her forehead.
Pointing with her finger, she counted out:

> *Eenie, meenie, meinie, mo,*
> *Catch a feenie, feinie, fo,*
> *If he hollers, let him go,*
> *Eenie, meenie, meinie, mo.*

She pointed last at Belinda.

Betsy took Belinda carefully from the shelf. She turned her around and around and looked at her beautiful clothes.

Belinda, tall and proud, stood on a little heart-shaped mirror. She wore a bride's dress of heavy white taffeta. Her skirt ended in a long train. On her black hair, she wore a long white veil. Tiny white flowers held her veil in place, and in her white-gloved hands she carried a bouquet of white roses. Tiny white shoes were fitted on her feet. Lace trimmed her white underthings, and every tuck and hemstitch had been made by careful hands.

"You are beautiful, Belinda," said Betsy, as she stood the doll on the shelf once more.

She walked across the room to her bed where Jennifer carelessly lay.

"I wish Susan was giving a prize for dolls like you, Jennifer," she said.

Jennifer smiled at her.

Again Betsy stood looking at Melissa, Belinda, and
Mary Jane. Then she counted out:

Engine, engine, number nine,
Running on Chicago line,
If she's polished she will shine,
Engine, engine, number nine.

She pointed last at Melissa.
She stood a minute looking at the oldest doll.

Melissa was made of wood. In spite of her age, her eyes shone brightly, and her cheeks were apple red. Her hair, still golden, but wispy with age, fell about her sharp shoulders. She wore a filmy white dress that was tied about the neck with a blue ribbon. She sat propped against little pillows in a cradle as old as she. A patchwork quilt covered her from the waist down.

At last, Betsy turned from the cradle.

She walked to the bed where Jennifer lay and stood looking at her. Then she shook her head sadly.

Jennifer smiled at her.

Again Betsy looked at Melissa, Belinda, and Mary Jane. Again she counted out:

> *Entry, kentry, cutry, corn,*
> *Apple seed and apple thorn.*
> *Wire, brier, limber lock,*
> *Three geese in a flock.*
> *One flew east, and one flew west,*
> *And one flew over the cuckoo's nest.*

She pointed last at Mary Jane.

Mary Jane was seated at a sewing machine. She wore a blue dress with a long, full skirt and long sleeves. About her neck she wore a black ribbon tied in a bow at her throat.

Betsy turned a key in Mary Jane's back. At once, Mary Jane's little feet began to work the treadle, and the sewing machine began to sew. Mary Jane leaned forward and watched the stitches. Then she raised herself from her chair, took the cloth in her hands, looked at it, and put it back in the machine again. As she sat down, her feet began to work the treadle, and the sewing machine began to sew. Over and over.

"Are you making Jennifer a dress, Mary Jane?" asked Betsy.

Mary Jane took the cloth in her hands and looked at it, slowly, as the key in her back unwound.

Jennifer smiled.

Betsy crossed the room to her bed.

She lifted Jennifer from the bed and looked at her.

Jennifer's wig was loose and her hair was tangled. Her nose was cracked. When Betsy tilted her, her left eye closed, but her right eye stayed open. Her cheeks were patched with adhesive tape. Her white stockings and her black patent leather slippers had been lost long ago, and her feet were bare. The toes on both her feet were worn away and her knees were scarred. But on her face she wore a smile that never went away.

"You aren't my oldest doll, Jennifer," said Betsy. "Your dress is a fright. And you can't do a single thing. But I do love you, dear Jennifer."

She carefully laid Jennifer back on the bed. For a minute she stood looking at her. She puckered her forehead.

Suddenly, she snatched Jennifer from the bed and rushed out of the room.

At five minutes before four, Betsy walked up the street to Susan's house. In her arms she carried Jennifer.

Jennifer still wore her faded blue dress, but it had been washed and ironed. She had clean patches of adhesive tape on her cheeks. Her cracked nose was scrubbed and shining. With the smile on her face that never went away, she looked like the happiest doll in the world.

Eleven guests came to Susan's party. Each of them brought a doll. Susan, too, brought a doll.

There was one old doll at the party. There were seven beautifully dressed dolls. There were three dolls who could do all kinds of things. And there was Jennifer.

Susan and her guests sat their dolls in a row on the sofa.

"They can watch us play games," said Susan.

Susan and her friends played musical chairs. They played treasure hunt. They pinned tails on a donkey.

"Now it is time for the prizes," said Susan's mother.

She laid three packages on the table. They were wrapped in pink paper and tied with blue ribbons. Beside them she set a small basket.

Susan and her guests took their dolls from the sofa—the old one, the beautifully dressed ones, those who could do all kinds of things, and Jennifer. The girls sat on the floor in a circle. They held their dolls in their arms and waited.

"Three dolls will be given special prizes," said Mrs. Anderson. "But all of them have made our party a happy one. I think each doll should have a small prize. Don't you?"

"Oh yes," answered the twelve girls.

From the basket Mrs. Anderson took twelve doll parasols. They were made of paper, with flowers of many colors printed on it. They opened and shut like real parasols.

Mrs. Anderson handed each girl a parasol for her doll.

"Oh!" said the girls. "Aren't they pretty?"

They opened and shut their parasols. They held them over their dolls.

"Thank you, Mrs. Anderson," they said.

Then they looked at the three packages lying on the table.

"Since only Anne has brought an old doll," said Mrs. Anderson, "her doll wins the prize as the oldest doll."

She took Anne's doll and held it up for all to see.

Anne's doll was not nearly as old as Melissa. She was only seventy years old.

Anne opened the package Mrs. Anderson handed her. In it was a Japanese doll wearing a gay flowered kimono with a bright orange-colored obi around her waist.

"Ah!" sighed the guests. "Isn't she pretty!"

"Thank you, Mrs. Anderson," said Anne. "Thank you very much."

Two packages were now left on the table.

"Now we shall choose the best-dressed doll," said Mrs. Anderson.

She walked back and forth in front of the seven beautifully dressed dolls.

The seven girls held up their dolls so Mrs. Anderson could see how well dressed they were. They watched Mrs. Anderson closely.

Betsy watched Mrs. Anderson for a minute. Then she looked at Jennifer. She kissed Jennifer on the nose.

Jennifer smiled at her.

"Laura," said Mrs. Anderson, "your doll wins the prize as the best-dressed doll."

Laura's doll was indeed well dressed. But she was not so beautifully dressed as Belinda. Her clothes had been bought at the store. None of them had been sewed by hand.

Laura opened the package Mrs. Anderson handed her. In it was an Indian doll wearing a green-and-gold sari.

"Ah!" sighed the guests. "Isn't she beautiful!"

"Thank you, Mrs. Anderson," said Laura. "Thank you very much."

One package was left on the table—only one.

"We have three dolls who can do things," said Mrs. Anderson. "Let's see what they can do."

One by one the three girls showed Mrs. Anderson all the things their dolls could do.

All the girls watched Mrs. Anderson.

Betsy watched her for a minute. Then she looked at Jennifer.

Jennifer smiled at her.

"This prize," said Mrs. Anderson, "goes to Sarah Page, because her doll can do the most things."

Sarah Page's doll could go to sleep. She could cry, and say *ma-ma*. But she couldn't sew a fine seam on a sewing machine.

Sarah Page opened the package Mrs. Anderson handed her. In it was a Hawaiian doll wearing a lei around her neck.

"Oh!" said the guests. "Isn't she fun!"

"Thank you, Mrs. Anderson," said Sarah Page. "Thank you very much."

Mrs. Anderson looked at all the dolls once more. She looked at Anne's old doll. She looked at the seven beautifully dressed dolls, and at the three dolls who could do all kinds of things. She looked at Jennifer.

Mrs. Anderson looked the longest at Jennifer.

Jennifer smiled at her.

"There will be one more prize," said Mrs. Anderson.

"Another prize?" said Susan. "What for?"

"For something important," said Mrs. Anderson. "Something I didn't think of before."

And she left the room.

Soon, Mrs. Anderson came back. In her hand she carried a round piece of gold paper the size of a silver dollar. Something was printed on it in big black letters.

"What is that?" asked the girls.

"It's a medal," said Mrs. Anderson.

She stooped before Jennifer and pinned the medal on the front of the doll's faded dress.

The guests crowded around to look.

"What does it say?" they asked.

"It says THE BEST-LOVED DOLL," said Mrs. Anderson.

"Ah!" sighed Nancy. "Just like my Amy. I almost brought Amy to the party."

Betsy kissed Jennifer on the nose again, loudly.

"Oh Mrs. Anderson," she said, "thank you. Thank you very much. Don't you want to thank Mrs. Anderson?" she said to Jennifer.

Jennifer smiled at Mrs. Anderson. As Betsy tilted the doll, she winked her left eye.

Mrs. Anderson invited the twelve girls and their dolls into the dining room. The girls sat around the dining table.

The twelve dolls sat on the floor around a low stool. The stool was set with Susan's blue willow doll dishes. At each of the twelve places was a tiny pink-frosted cupcake. Beside each cupcake was a tiny doll fan.

The twelve girls ate big pink-frosted cupcakes and drank pink lemonade. They opened their dolls' parasols. They twirled them around and shut them. They talked and laughed. They looked at their dolls.

"Doesn't Jennifer look happy wearing her medal?" asked Nancy.

"I believe she knows she's won it," said Sarah Page.

"She does," said Betsy.

At last the guests gathered their dolls in their arms. They took the parasols and the doll cupcakes and the doll fans, and started home.

"Good-bye, Susan," they said. "Good-bye, Mrs. Anderson. Thank you for the party." And away they went, along the street, some one way, some another.